THE WORLD'S TOP TEN

DESERTS

Neil Morris

ILLUSTRATED BY VANESSA CARD

❧ Belitha Press

Words in **bold** are explained in the glossary
on pages 30–31.

First published in the UK in 1996
by Belitha Press Limited
London House, Great Eastern Wharf
Parkgate Road, London SW11 4NQ

Copyright in this format © Belitha Press 1996
Text copyright © Neil Morris 1996
Illustrations copyright © Vanessa Card 1996

ISBN 1 85561 512 6

British Library Cataloguing in Publication Data
for this book is available from the British Library.

Editor: Claire Edwards
Designer: Dawn Apperley
Picture researcher: Juliet Duff
Consultant: Elizabeth M Lewis

Printed in Hong Kong

Picture acknowledgements: J. Allen Cash Ltd: 15.
FLPA: 12 Eric & David Hosking, 21, 26 D. Hall, 29 top
C. Carvalho. Hutchison Library: 5 bottom, 13,
18 Christina Dodwell, 19 Dave Brinicombe, 28 top.
Images of Africa: 29 bottom. Images of India: 27. NHPA:
11 ANT, 16 Nigel J. Dennis, 22 Peter Johnson, 24 Anthony
Bannister, 28 bottom David Middleton. Still Pictures: 5 top
Cyril Ruoso, 8 Frans Lemmens, 9 Bios/George Lopez,
14 Stephen Pern, 17 Bios/Martin Gilles, 23 Foto
Natura/Martin Harvey. Tony Stone Images: 10 Ken
Stepnell. Telegraph Colour Library: 20. Trip: 25 T. Noorits.

Contents

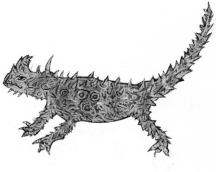

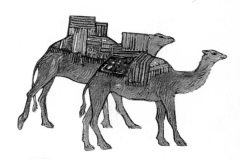

What is a desert?

A desert is an area of land where very little rain falls.
This means that the ground is dry nearly all the time.
Most deserts are in warm parts of the world, and we often
think of them as being covered with endless sand **dunes**.
But there are many other desert **landscapes**, including rocky
hills and flat stony plains. There is no single definition, but
most scientists agree that any region that has less than
25 centimetres of rain a year can be called a desert.

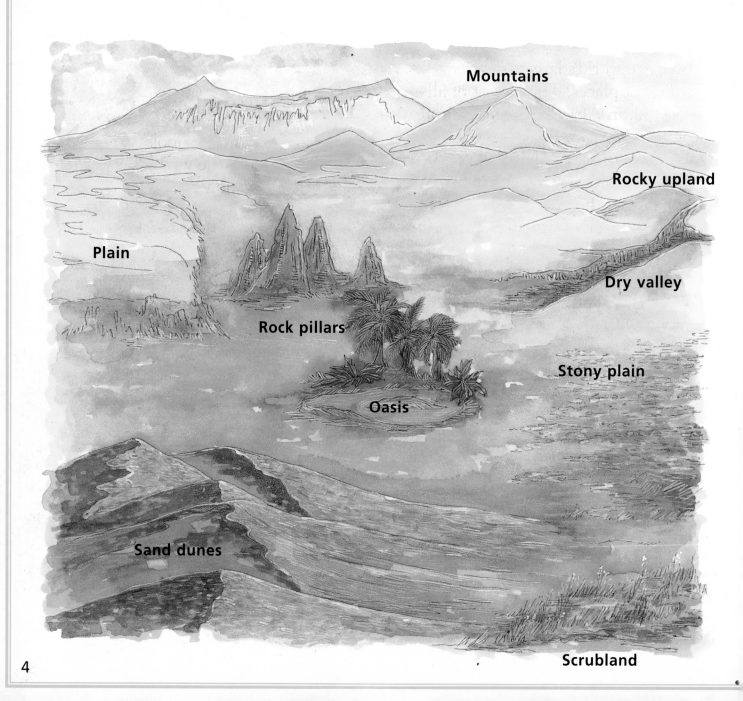

Mountains

Rocky upland

Plain

Dry valley

Rock pillars

Stony plain

Oasis

Sand dunes

Scrubland

Hot deserts

Most of the world's largest deserts are very hot places. The largest of all, the Sahara, in Africa, has temperatures that reach 50°C. In hot deserts the temperature usually falls very fast at night, sometimes by as much as 25°C.

Despite their heat, temperature changes and lack of water, deserts are not empty wastelands. Many kinds of plants and animals live in this difficult **environment**, and some people live in deserts too.

This dry, rocky area is a typical desert landscape in the Negev region of southern Israel.

The biggest deserts

In this book we take a look at the ten biggest deserts in the world. We see where they are, how different they are from each other, and learn something of the people and animals who have made the desert their home.

Cold wilderness

Not all deserts are as hot as the Sahara. The Gobi, in Mongolia, is very cold indeed in winter. The two **polar** regions, the Arctic and Antarctic, can also be called deserts. These areas are so cold that there is little rainfall and any moisture instantly freezes. The icy wastes around the North and South Poles get bigger in the winter and smaller in the summer.

Baking heat in summer and freezing cold in winter have helped shape the stony hills of the Gobi, the world's fourth largest desert.

The biggest deserts

This map shows the ten biggest deserts in the world. Although we show them clearly on the map, the edges of a desert are not as clear as the borders of a country or the coastline of an island. Many of the world's deserts are growing very slowly. This process is called **desertification**.

The world's top ten deserts

1	Sahara	8 400 000 sq km
2	Australian	1 550 000 sq km
3	Arabian	1 300 000 sq km
4	Gobi	1 040 000 sq km
5	Kalahari	520 000 sq km
6	Takla Makan	320 000 sq km
7	Sonoran	310 000 sq km
8	Namib	300 000 sq km
9	Kara Kum	270 000 sq km
10	Thar	260 000 sq km

NORTH AMERICA

Sonoran

ATLANTIC OCEAN

SOUTH AMERICA

PACIFIC OCEAN

Sahara

The Sahara is by far the biggest desert in the world. It stretches over 5000 kilometres from the Atlantic Ocean to the Red Sea, and covers more than a quarter of the continent of Africa. Its name comes from an Arabic word for desert.

MEDITERRANEAN SEA

ATLANTIC OCEAN

Scorpion

Locust

River Nile

RED SEA

Falcon

Ahaggar Mountains

Sandgrouse

Tuareg people

Oasis

Jerboa

Fennec fox

Arabian camels

Desert hedgehog

Addax

Seas of sand

Some parts of the Sahara are made up of kilometre after kilometre of shifting sand dunes. These huge areas of continuous sand are called **ergs**, and in these areas many dunes are more than 200 metres high. The world's highest sand dunes are in the Algerian part of the Sahara. They are 465 metres high, which is taller than the Empire State Building in New York.

Winds blow the sand dunes of the Sahara into all sorts of different shapes.

Some peaks of the Ahaggar Mountains, in southern Algeria, are nearly 3000 metres high.

Rocks and mountains

Only about a fifth of the Sahara is covered with sand. Some of the desert is made up of flat stony plains called **regs**. At its lowest point, the desert is 132 metres below sea level. But most of the Sahara is made up of rocky uplands called **hammadas**, and there are many high mountains. At the Sahara's highest point in Chad, the Tibesti Mountains rise to 3415 metres. These mountainous regions have slightly more rain than other parts of the desert, and there is sometimes snow on the peaks.

Wandering the desert

The Sahara has about 90 large **fertile** areas, called **oases**, where people live in villages and grow crops. There are also many smaller oases that support one or two families each.

Altogether, fewer than 2 million people live in the Sahara. Many of these are **nomads**, such as the Tuareg of the central uplands. Nomadic people wander the desert, travelling from one oasis to the next.

FACTS

AREA 8 400 000 sq km

LOCATION MAP

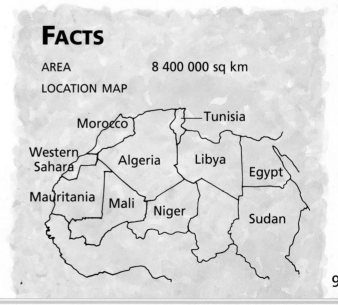

Morocco · Tunisia · Western Sahara · Algeria · Libya · Egypt · Mauritania · Mali · Niger · Sudan

9

Australian

We use the name Australian Desert to refer to five desert areas that spread across western and central Australia. They are the Great Sandy, Great Victoria, Simpson, Gibson and Sturt Deserts. These vast desert areas are linked, as the map shows.

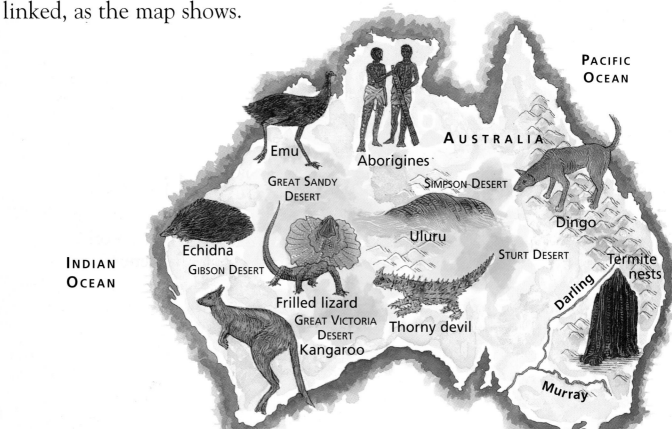

PACIFIC OCEAN

AUSTRALIA

Emu

Aborigines

GREAT SANDY DESERT

SIMPSON DESERT

Dingo

Echidna

GIBSON DESERT

Uluru

STURT DESERT

Termite nests

INDIAN OCEAN

Frilled lizard

GREAT VICTORIA DESERT

Thorny devil

Kangaroo

Darling

Murray

Desert continent

Deserts cover more than a third of Australia, making it the world's driest continent. But the Australian Desert has a little more rainfall than most other desert regions. This means that many areas have a thin cover of **vegetation**. In years of good rainfall, these areas are used for grazing sheep. In Australia, **bush** areas with shrubs and some trees are called the **outback**.

This part of the Simpson Desert has a good covering of shrubs and trees.

FACTS

AREA   1 550 000 sq km

LOCATION   Australia: between
              the Indian and the
              Pacific Oceans

These Aboriginal children have put on body paint for a dance festival. Many Aborigine customs and ceremonies are thousands of years old.

The first Australians

The Aborigines came to Australia from Asia about 40 000 years ago. They probably crossed land that is now under water, and wandered the desert, hunting and gathering food. Their traditional way of life was threatened when settlers arrived from Europe in the eighteenth century. Now some areas of desert have been set aside as Aboriginal **reserves**.

Runners and jumpers

Many animals in the Australian Desert live nowhere else in the world. Early European explorers were so surprised by emus and kangaroos that they described Australia as the land where birds run instead of flying and animals hop instead of running. The emu is a large bird, but it has small wings and cannot fly. It is as tall as a man and can run faster than a world-champion sprinter. The red kangaroo is even taller and hops along on its huge back legs. It can clear more than 9 metres in one bound.

Arabian

The Arabian Desert covers nearly all of the Arabian **Peninsula**. This peninsula, in south-west Asia, is separated from Africa and the Sahara by the Red Sea. The desert covers parts of five countries and is made up of three different desert areas, called Rub' al Khali, An Nafud and the Syrian Desert.

MEDITERRANEAN SEA

SYRIAN DESERT

Date palms

UNITED ARAB EMIRATES

PERSIAN GULF

Wild ass

Bedouin camp

JORDAN

SAUDI ARABIA

AN NAFUD

Oil

Oryx

RUB' AL KHALI

Arabian camel

RED SEA

OMAN

YEMEN

GULF OF ADEN

This part of the empty quarter, in northern Yemen, shows clearly how this desert region got its name.

The Empty Quarter

The desert region called Rub' al Khali, in southern Saudi Arabia, is one of the largest stretches of sand in the world. Its name means 'empty quarter'. It is so hot and dry that very few people ever go into this wilderness, though some **Bedouin** nomads wander along its edges.

A desert's sand forms over millions of years. As rocks are heated rapidly during the day they **expand**. As they cool rapidly at night they **contract**. Gradually they begin to crumble and form sand, which is then blown about the desert by the wind. In the Arabian Desert, strong winds from the north carry and move huge loads of sand and dust, constantly changing the landscape.

Ship of the desert

The one-humped camel of the Arabian Peninsula is called a **dromedary**. This large, strong animal is well-suited to life in the desert. Camels store fat in their humps and can go for days without food or water. The fat provides them with energy, and as they use it, their humps shrink. The dromedary is the main form of transport across a sea of sand. Because of this, it is often called 'the ship of the desert'.

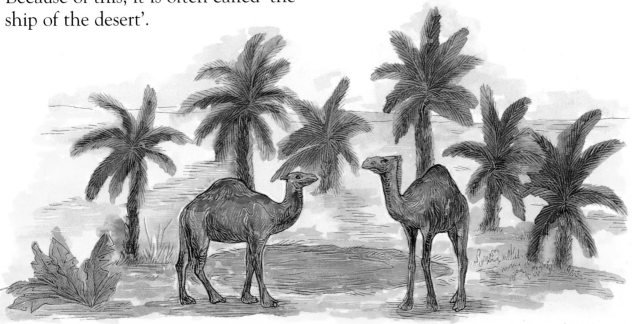

An oil refinery in the Arabian Desert. Most of the oil fields are near the Gulf coast. Oil and natural gas are the region's main resources.

Oil beneath the sands

Oil is a very important **resource**, and is sometimes trapped in the layers of rock beneath a desert. The discovery of oil in the Arabian Desert brought wealth and many changes to the countries in the region. The largest of these, Saudi Arabia, is the third biggest producer of **crude oil** in the world.

After the oil has been brought to the surface, it is pumped through pipelines to huge ships, called tankers, on the coast of the Persian Gulf. The tankers then carry it to other countries around the world.

Gobi

The Gobi Desert stretches across the borders of Mongolia and China, in central Asia. Its name comes from a Mongolian word meaning 'waterless place'. This desert is the furthest north and generally the coldest of the ten big deserts. It lies on a **plateau**, between 900 and 1500 metres high.

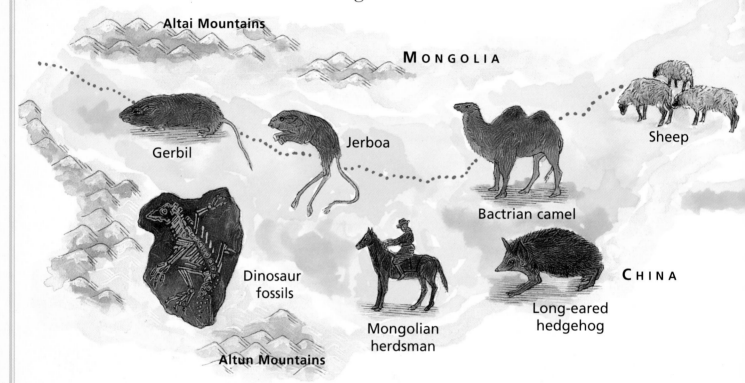

Altai Mountains

MONGOLIA

Gerbil

Jerboa

Sheep

Bactrian camel

Dinosaur fossils

Mongolian herdsman

Long-eared hedgehog

CHINA

Altun Mountains

Extreme cold and heat

The Gobi Desert has extreme weather. In winter the temperature drops to -40°C. Spring and autumn are dry and cold. But in the summer there are long heat waves, and the temperature can rise to 45°C in July. The desert's small amount of rain falls mainly in the warmer months and **evaporates** quickly. This severe climate has created a rocky wasteland surrounded by dry grasslands called **steppes**. There are some high sand dunes in the Gobi, too.

A Mongolian boy herds his cattle across grassland at the edge of the desert.

Land of the dinosaurs

Scientists think that the Gobi may once have had a less severe climate. We now know that dinosaurs roamed this area millions of years ago. In the 1920s an American scientist went into the desert in search of eagles' nests. He found the nests, and also came across some **fossilized** dinosaur eggs that were 95 million years old. This was the first proof that dinosaurs laid eggs. Since then there have been many successful fossil-hunting expeditions in the Gobi. Parts of a giant dinosaur, Deinocheirus, were found there.

The Mongolian Valley of the Dinosaurs, where many **prehistoric** bones have been found. It is hard work searching and digging in this barren region, and fossil-hunters have to take all their water with them.

Camels and horses

The Bactrian camel of the Gobi has two humps on its back. It has a long, woolly coat to keep it warm in winter. In summer most of this hair falls out. Some Bactrian camels are wild, but most are kept by nomads and herdsmen as working animals.

The Mongols of northern China and Mongolia are expert horse riders. They follow their herds of sheep, goats and cattle across the desert and surrounding steppes.

FACTS

AREA	1 040 000 sq km
LOCATION	central Asia: southern Mongolia and northern China

Kalahari

The Kalahari is a large dry **plain** in southern Africa. It covers most of Botswana, and spreads into parts of neighbouring Namibia and South Africa. Some parts of the Kalahari have more than the usual amount of rain for a desert, especially in the summer. Because of this, there are large areas of grassland and **scrub** within the region.

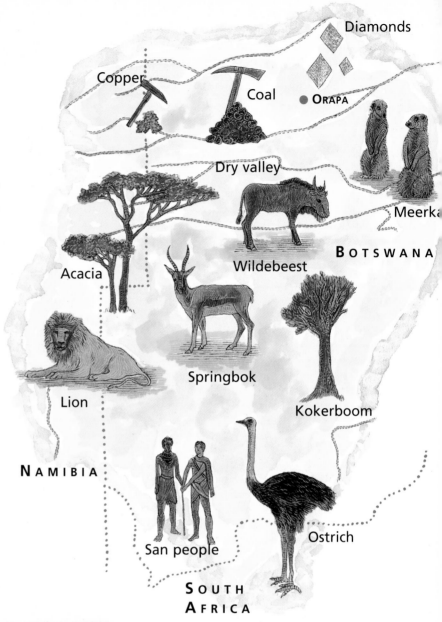

Diamonds

Copper

Coal

ORAPA

Dry valley

Meerka

Acacia

Wildebeest

BOTSWANA

Springbok

Lion

Kokerboom

NAMIBIA

San people

Ostrich

SOUTH
AFRICA

Dry valleys

In the northern part of the Kalahari, ancient river valleys can still be seen. In the south, four more dry valleys – the Auob, Kuruman, Molopo and Nossob – wind their way towards the flowing Orange River. These sandy river beds are like phantoms. Water only flows along them during the **rainy season** in exceptionally wet years.

Some trees manage to survive in the grassland regions of the Kalahari, where there is sometimes rain.

Life in the bush

The San people, or Bushmen, of the Kalahari are nomadic **hunter-gatherers**. They once spread across most of southern Africa, but today there are probably fewer than 2000 San living a traditional life in the desert. They are expert at desert survival. The men are skilful hunters, using arrows tipped with poison made from beetles. San women and children spend much of their time gathering plants. San children quickly learn to recognize and name 200 different plants.

A young San boy tends his fire. Traditionally, these desert-dwellers make shelters from branches thatched with dry grasses.

FACTS

AREA	520 000 sq km
LOCATION	southern Africa: parts of Botswana, Namibia and South Africa

The changing desert

In the Kalahari Gemsbok **National Park**, acacia trees grow in the dry river beds. Grass and shrubs provide food for herds of antelopes and wildebeest. There are also lions, smaller cats, wild dogs, jackals, meerkats, ostriches and many other birds. This is a **protected** area for wildlife, but in other parts of the Kalahari, companies have found coal, copper and other **minerals**. One of the largest diamond mines in the world is at Orapa, in northern Botswana.

Takla Makan

The sixth biggest desert in the world has a name that means: 'Go in, and you won't come out again'. The Takla Makan lies in the Xinjiang province of north-west China.

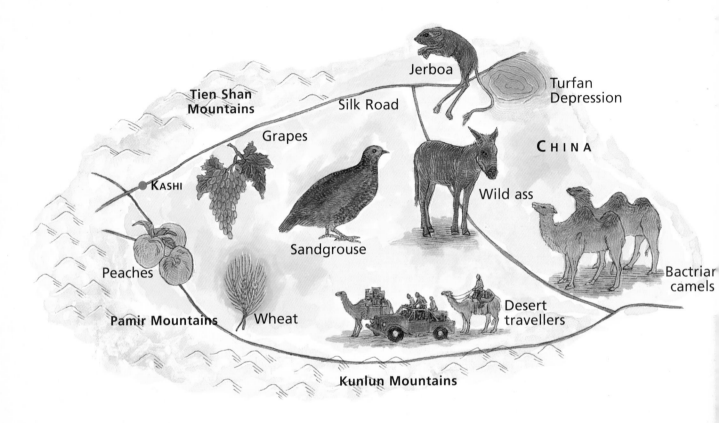

- Jerboa
- Tien Shan Mountains
- Silk Road
- Turfan Depression
- Grapes
- CHINA
- KASHI
- Wild ass
- Sandgrouse
- Peaches
- Bactrian camels
- Pamir Mountains
- Wheat
- Desert travellers
- Kunlun Mountains

The snow-capped Pamir Mountains form a backdrop to the stony wastes of the desert.

High mountains

The Takla Makan reaches a height of 1500 metres, and is surrounded on three sides by mountain ranges. In the north the snow-capped Tien Shan, or Heavenly Mountains, separate China from Kyrgyzstan. To the south the Kunlun Mountains divide the desert from Xizang province, while in the west there are the high Pamir Mountains.

In the east, 153 metres below sea level, lies a great bowl of dry rock. This is the Turfan Depression, the second lowest hollow in the surface of the Earth.

Ancient Silk Road

The famous Italian explorer Marco Polo travelled over the Pamir Mountains and round the southern edges of the Takla Makan, at the end of the thirteenth century. He journeyed with his father and his uncle in a **caravan** of camels, horses and donkeys. They followed the Silk Road.

This was the ancient trade route used by merchants to take valuable silk from China to Europe.

In the desert the Polos put up a sign at night, pointing in the direction they were travelling. In the morning, although the landscape looked the same all around them, they knew which way to go.

Mud-brick ruins near the Turfan Depression are all that remain of the town of Gaochang. This was once an important stop for camel caravans on the ancient Silk Road.

Oasis city

Kashi, at the western end of the desert and at the foot of the Pamir Mountains, grew up around an oasis. It was an important stop for caravans on the ancient Silk Road and has been fought over by many different peoples. The Chinese first occupied Kashi in the second century BC, and in 1219 it was won by the Mongols. There are still silk markets in the city (see above).

Kashi is very fertile. It is supplied with water by a river and a series of wells. Wheat, maize and rice are grown there, as well as melons, grapes and peaches.

FACTS

AREA	320 000 sq km
LOCATION	north-west China: Xinjiang Uygur province

Sonoran

North America's biggest desert is the seventh largest in the world. The Sonoran Desert runs across the border between the United States and Mexico. It covers parts of two American states, Arizona and California, as well as three Mexican states, including Sonora.

Desert tortoise

Papago Indian

USA

PHOENIX

Colorado

Cottontail

Elf owl

Gila woodpecker

TUCSON

PACIFIC OCEAN

Gila monster

Saguaro

MEXICO

Yucca

Roadrunner

GULF OF CALIFORNIA

Rattlesnake

The modern city of Phoenix, Arizona, stands on ancient Indian desert lands. Here the ancestors of Papago and Pima Indians built canals to help them farm the land.

Region of contrasts

The Sonoran Desert has many different forms of landscape. There are large areas of sand dunes, cactus forests, rocky wastes, Indian **reservations** and national parks. A big road runs across the northern part of the desert. This is called **Interstate highway** 10.

It links the city of Tucson with Phoenix, the state capital of Arizona. Tucson has a population of 430 000, and Phoenix has over 2 million people. There are many other smaller towns within the desert region. These townspeople are modern desert-dwellers.

Traditional desert people

Native Americans have lived in this area for 20 000 years. Traditionally, five of these Indian tribal groups lived as herders and farmers in the Sonoran Desert. They are the Maricopa, Mohave, Papago, Pima and Yuma Indians.

Today, 6000 native Americans live on the Papago Reservation. They lead a modern life, but have not forgotten their traditional roots. They call themselves Tohono O'odham, or 'desert people'. When they lived by gathering food from the desert, their most important yearly festival was a rainmaking ceremony. Other tribes have their own ceremonies, such as the deer dance of the Yaqui Indians.

FACTS

AREA	310 000 sq km
LOCATION	south-west North America: Arizona and California, USA; Baja California, Baja California Sur and Sonora, Mexico.

Giant cactus

The Sonoran Desert has 300 different types of cactus, including the saguaro, which is the largest in the world. This giant can grow over 17 metres tall – about the height of nine men. Some desert birds find the cactus useful. Gila woodpeckers peck their way into saguaros to make their nest. And when they leave, the tiny elf owl takes its turn in the ready-made hole.

The roadrunner, on the other hand, spends its time on the ground. This bird, a relative of the cuckoo, runs away from danger and will chase anything that moves. It can sprint at speeds of up to 24 kph.

Tall saguaros grow among other cactuses, grasses and shrubs in many parts of the Sonoran Desert.

21

Namib

The Namib Desert runs in a long strip along the Atlantic coast of Namibia, in southern Africa. It is just a few hundred kilometres west of the Kalahari Desert. The Namib is one of the world's oldest deserts, dating back 55 million years or more.

Antelope

SKELETON COAST

NAMIBIA

Sidewinding viper

Shipwreck

ATLANTIC OCEAN

Sand lizard

Darkling beetle

Welwitschia

Orange River

Skeleton Coast

The northern coastline of the Namib Desert is called the Skeleton Coast. Its name comes from the huge number of shipwrecks that have happened there. Thick fog, dangerous ocean **currents**, howling gales, hidden **reefs** and rocks have caused these disasters. Stories are told of sailors scrambling ashore, only to die in the dry, hot desert.

A shipwreck shows why this is called the Skeleton Coast. The desert sands are constantly moving, and soon bury anything that is washed up by the sea.

The Namib's inland dunes are formed by sand carried from the coast by fierce winds. Trees have sent deep roots down to find water even here. This may be the beginning of a small oasis.

Blooming desert

The strange welwitschia plant, which grows only on gravel plains in the Namib, can live for more than a thousand years. It has a huge, 3-metre-long root and two long leaves that look like frayed straps. It takes in moisture through millions of **pores** and stores this in its root. Other desert plants have a very short life. When it rains, they suddenly shoot up. They flower within a few weeks and scatter their seeds before they die.

Sea fog

The Namib has very little rain, but on many days fog rolls in from the sea. The fog is caused by cold-water currents in the ocean cooling the warm air above. This gives the desert some moisture, which helps a number of small animals to survive. Beetles, termites and spiders depend on the fog for water. The fog collects on their bodies and turns to dew. Lizards find their moisture by eating the insects, and they in turn are eaten by the desert viper. This poisonous **sidewinding** viper hunts by burying itself in the sand and waiting for prey.

FACTS

AREA	300 000 sq km
LOCATION	south-west Africa: along the Atlantic coast of Namibia

23

Kara Kum

The Kara Kum, or 'black desert', is in the western part of central Asia. It lies in Turkmenistan, a country on the Caspian Sea that became independent in 1991 when the Soviet Union split up.

ARAL SEA

Oil

Gas

TURKMENISTAN

Lizard

Bactrian camel

Carpet

CASPIAN SEA

Amu Darya

Goat

Wild ass

Cotton

ASHKHABAD

Sheep

Karakumsky Canal

Kopet Dag Mountains

Desert republic

The Kara Kum covers more than half the republic of Turkmenistan. At the south-west corner of the desert, the Kopet Dag mountain range forms the border with Iran. These rugged mountains tower over the Turkmenistan capital city, Ashkhabad. Local people call the **foothills** moon mountains, because they are almost completely bare. Violent earthquakes shake this region and are gradually pushing the mountains higher.

The barren peaks of the Kopet Dag mountains rise up at the edge of the desert.

Industry and agriculture

The Kara Kum is rich in oil and natural gas, and the region's chemical and mining industries have grown in recent years. In the oases people grow cotton and raise sheep and horses. The local karakul sheep have black, grey or brown coats. Wool from the lambs is especially valuable.

Irrigation has created oases and helped farmers. The biggest waterway is the Karakumsky Canal. It runs more than 1000 kilometres from the River Amu Darya to the foothills of the Kopet Dag mountains.

Flocks of karakul sheep are herded by Turkmen people, mainly for their lambs. The curly fur of karakul lambs is often called Persian lamb.

Turkmen people

The Turkmen were once nomadic people. They lived in dome-shaped tents and wandered the edges of the Kara Kum. A few still live for part of the year in tents, moving when they need to find new land to graze their herds of goats, sheep and camels. They are Muslims, followers of the religion of Islam.

Turkmen are famous for making carpets with beautiful designs. Many of the carpets are now woven in factories, and are important to the **economy** of Turkmenistan.

FACTS

AREA	270 000 sq km
LOCATION	west central Asia: Turkmenistan

25

Thar

The Thar, also called the Great Indian Desert, is a region of rolling sand hills in north-west India and Pakistan. It is the tenth biggest desert in the world, and covers most of the Indian state of Rajasthan.

Gazelle

Rajasthan Canal

PAKISTAN

Great bustard

BIKANER

JAISALMER

Camel safari

Wild ass

INDIA

ARABIAN SEA

Rajasthan people

The desert town of Jaisalmer, viewed from the top of the town's old fort. Hindu warriors built many forts in Rajasthan hundreds of years ago.

Watering the desert

There is little water in the Thar Desert. Almost all the year's rain falls in just three months, from July to September. Rainwater is collected in tanks and **reservoirs**, and many canals have been built to take water across the desert. The biggest is the Rajasthan Canal. It carries water 649 kilometres from the north and irrigates the areas around the desert towns of Bikaner and Jaisalmer. When there is water, farmers grow crops such as wheat, cotton and sugar cane. But there are often severe droughts.

Travel by camel

There are railways and dusty roads across the Thar Desert, but many local people prefer to travel by camel. Visitors to Jaisalmer can go on a camel expedition into the desert. The 300-kilometre trek to Bikaner takes 11 days. There is usually one camel per person, plus one each for luggage. Desert riders on these treks need to take water bottles, suntan lotion, a large hat, sunglasses and a soft cushion to sit on. At Jaisalmer there is also a Desert Festival every February, with camel races and camel polo.

FACTS

AREA	260 000 sq km
LOCATION	Indian subcontinent: across the Rajasthan state in India; the Sind province in Pakistan

Rajasthani women collect firewood. Irrigation canals have helped plants to grow in the Thar region, but wood.is still scarce.

The spreading desert

Over the last 10 000 years, the Thar Desert has been growing. This may be because of changes in the local climate, especially the wind direction. But people have also helped to speed up the growth of the desert. For example, in the 1970s many of the forests in India, in the areas around the desert, were cut down. Once trees have gone, the unsheltered soil dries quickly and is blown away by the wind.

The world's deserts

The world's main hot deserts are found in two bands that stretch right around the Earth. One band is north of the **Equator** and follows the line of the **Tropic** of Cancer. This includes the Sahara and the Arabian Deserts. The other band lies along the Tropic of Capricorn, and this includes the Australian and the Kalahari Deserts. As well as the ten biggest, there are many other deserts in the world.

Atacama

The Atacama Desert (right) stretches for almost 1000 kilometres along the Pacific coast of northern Chile, in South America. It covers an area of 180 000 square kilometres and is probably the driest region on Earth. Few plants grow here, and the wind-blown landscape is covered with salt, left behind as moisture evaporates.

Mojave

The Mojave Desert, in southern California, USA, blooms in spring (left). A beavertail cactus shows its beautiful flowers, though these will not last for very long. The Mojave, which covers an area of about 35 000 square kilometres, is almost completely surrounded by mountains. To its north is Death Valley, the hottest and driest place in North America. In some parts of the desert, people driving trucks have caused dust-storms over 30 kilometres long. To the south is another dry area, the Colorado Desert. The world's largest solar-power plant is in the Mojave Desert.

Antarctica

The continent of Antarctica (above), around the South Pole, is sometimes called an ice desert. This white wasteland is more than one and a half times the size of the Sahara Desert. A thick **ice sheet** covers the region, which is the coldest and windiest place on Earth.

The average temperature in parts of the Antarctic is -58°C. In winter, gales blow across the ice at up to 320 kilometres an hour. No one lives permanently in Antarctica, though there are several scientific bases. The region is protected by an international treaty.

East Africa

Life is hard for the people of the desert regions of northern Kenya (left), Somalia and Ethiopia. The area has very few plants, and in recent years East African countries have been hit by terrible droughts and famines. The Somali Desert is the eleventh biggest in the world. In Somalia, civil war has made life in the desert even harder.

29

Glossary

Bedouin Arab nomads who wander the Arabian Desert and parts of the Sahara.

bush Land partly covered with shrubs and some trees.

caravan A group travelling together.

contract To become smaller.

crude oil Oil before it has been treated in a refinery.

current A strong, steady flow of water in one direction.

desertification The process of fertile land becoming desert.

dromedary A one-humped Arabian camel.

Kangaroos in their desert environment.

Tuareg crossing the desert on their camels.

dune A high mound of sand.

economy A country's wealth, and how it uses its resources, goods and services.

environment The surroundings in which people, animals or plants live.

Equator An imaginary circle around the middle of the Earth.

erg An area of shifting sand dunes.

evaporate To change from a liquid to a vapour.

expand To grow bigger.

fertile Having rich soil and producing good crops.

foothills The lower slopes of a mountain.

fossilize To preserve the remains of once-living things from prehistoric times.

hammada An area of rocky upland.

hunter-gatherers People who live by hunting wild animals and gathering fruit, roots and berries.

ice sheet A thick layer of ice covering a large area of land.

Interstate highway A long main road that runs between American states.

irrigation Watering the land using canals and ditches.

landscape An area of land and its special features.

mineral Any natural, solid material found in the earth that does not come from plants or animals.

national park An area that people visit where animals and plants are protected.

nomads People who wander from place to place to find food and grazing land for their animals.

oasis An area in a desert with water, where plants can grow and people live.

outback The bush country of Australia.

peninsula A strip of land that juts into a sea; it is almost an island.

plain Flat countryside with few trees.

plateau A flat area of high land.

polar Near the North or South Pole.

pore A tiny opening.

prehistoric Relating to ancient times before writing was invented.

protected Looked after and kept from harm.

rainy season The time of year when a great deal of rain falls.

Camels arriving at an oasis in the desert.

reef A ridge of rock, sand or coral near the surface of the sea.

reg A flat stony plain.

reservation An area of land set aside for American Indian people.

reserve An area set aside for particular people, and to protect the plants and animals that live there.

reservoir A large lake used to collect and store water.

resource Something that people can use to live on, or that can bring wealth when sold to others.

Lions resting in the desert scrub.

scrub An area of scattered bushes, small trees and other plants in a dry region.

sidewinding Moving forwards with a sideways, looping motion.

steppe An area of grassy plains.

tropic One of the two imaginary circles around the Earth, one above and one below the Equator. Between the two is the hottest part of the Earth.

vegetation All plant life.

Index

Words in **bold** appear in the glossary on pages 30-31.